MW00562996

Ladybird Readers

The Tortoise and the Hare

Series Editor: Sorrel Pitts
Text adapted by Nicole Irving
Activities written by Catrin Morris
Illustrated by Irina Golina-Sagatelian

LADYBIRD BOOKS

UK | USA | Canada | Ireland | Australia
India | New Zealand | South Africa

Ladybird Books is part of the Penguin Random House group of companies
whose addresses can be found at global.penguinrandomhouse.com.
www.penguin.co.uk   www.puffin.co.uk   www.ladybird.co.uk

Penguin
Random House
UK

First published 2020
001

Copyright © Ladybird Books Ltd, 2020

Printed in China

A CIP catalogue record for this book is available from the British Library

ISBN: 978–0–241–40173–6

All correspondence to:
Ladybird Books
Penguin Random House Children's
80 Strand, London WC2R ORL

MIX
Paper from
responsible sources
FSC
www.fsc.org
FSC® C018179

The Tortoise and the Hare

Picture words

Tortoise

Hare

Fox

slow   fast

grass

smile

race

jump

win

"Look at me," says Hare.

"Well done," says Fox.

6

"What are you doing?"
asks Tortoise.

"I am jumping," says Hare.

"Oh!" says Tortoise.

"Yes," says Hare. "I can jump, and I can run fast."

"Can you jump, Tortoise?"
asks Hare.

"No, I can't," says Tortoise.

"Oh," says Hare.

"Can you run,
Tortoise?" asks Hare.

"No, I can't," says Tortoise.

"Oh," says Hare.

"But I can walk,"
says Tortoise.

"Haha, you can walk!"
says Hare, and smiles.

"Yes. I'm a tortoise,"
says Tortoise.
"I can walk."

"Then we can't have
a race," says Hare.

"Why not?" asks Tortoise.

"You are too slow,"
says Hare.

"Me, too slow? Then let's have a race," says Tortoise.

"OK! Let's run from here to the beach," says Hare.

"Great," says Tortoise.

"Put your feet here,"
says Fox.

"Three, two, one, GO!"

"Hare is fast . . ." says Fox.

"Tortoise is slow," says Hare.
"I can eat this nice grass."

"Now I can sit and enjoy the sun," says Hare.

"Oh," says Tortoise.
"Hare is sleeping!"

"Well done, Tortoise!"
says Fox. "Where's Hare?"

"Oh," says Hare. "You are slow, but you CAN win a race!"

Activities

The key below describes the skills practiced in each activity.

🖊 Spelling and writing

📖 Reading

💬 Speaking

❓ Critical thinking

✳ Preparation for the Cambridge Young Learners exams

1 Match the words to the pictures.

1 fast

2 grass

3 jump

4 race

5 slow

6 win

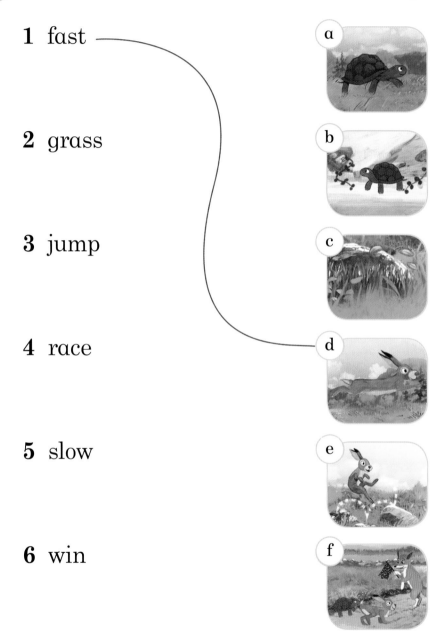

2 **Look and read. Put a** ✓ **or a** ✗
in the boxes. 📖 ⭐

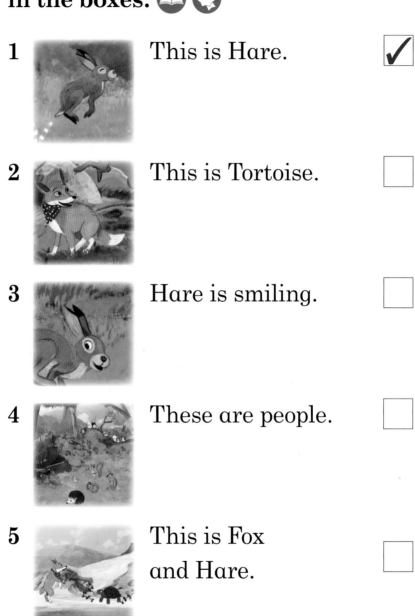

1   This is Hare.   ✓

2   This is Tortoise.   ☐

3   Hare is smiling.   ☐

4   These are people.   ☐

5   This is Fox
     and Hare.   ☐

3 Who says this?

Hare   Tortoise   Fox

1 "Look at me,"

    says _____ Hare _____.

2 "Well done,"

    says _____.

3 "What are you doing?"

    says _____.

4 "I am jumping,"

    says _____.

5 "But I can walk,"

    says _____.

4 **Complete the sentences.**
Write a—e. 📖

1 Look at   ....c.......

2 Well   ....

3 What are   ....

4 I am   ....

5 I can   ....

a done.

b jumping.

c me.

d run fast.

e you doing?

5 **Read the text and choose the correct words.**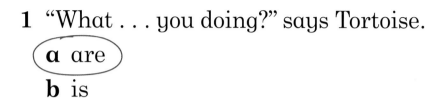

1 "What . . . you doing?" says Tortoise.

a are

b is

2 "I . . . jumping," says Hare.

a am

b are

3 "Oh!" . . . Tortoise.

a say

b says

4 "I can . . . fast."

a run

b runs

6 **Work with a friend. You are Hare. Your friend is Tortoise. Ask and answer questions.** 🗨

"Can you jump, Tortoise?" asks Hare.

"No, I can't," says Tortoise. "Oh," says Hare.

Can you jump?

No, I can't.

Can you run fast?

Can you walk?

7 Circle the correct words.

"Can you run, Tortoise?" asks Hare.

"No, I can't," says Tortoise.

"Oh," says Hare.

"But I can walk," says Tortoise.

1 Hare asks Tortoise,

    a "Can you eat grass?"

    b "Can you jump?"

2 Tortoise says,

    a "No, I can't."

    b "Yes, I can."

3 Then, Hare asks Tortoise,

    a "Can you run?"

    b "Can you walk?"

4 Tortoise says,

    a "But I can run."

    b "But I can walk."

8 **Read the sentences and match them with the correct animal. Write 1—3.** 📖 ❂

1 This animal can run very fast.

2 This animal is slow.

3 This animal has white feet.

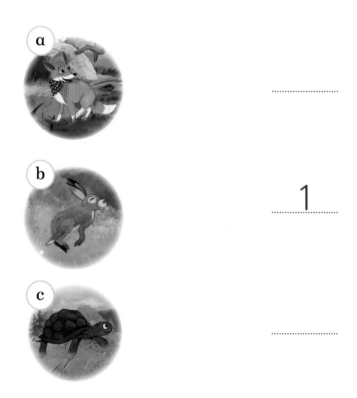

a ....

b ___1___

c ....

9 **Look at the letters.**
Write the words.

1  u p m j

j u m p

2  m i l e s

....

3  k a l w

....

4  s a g r s

....

5 w o l s

....

10 Find the words. 📖

a	h	r	e	s	a	t	a	w
d	r	a	r	s	l	o	w	p
a	b	c	j	m	e	r	f	i
j	f	e	w	i	n	t	h	b
u	i	j	k	l	f	o	t	m
m	n	o	p	e	a	i	q	l
p	r	s	t	u	s	s	v	e
w	x	s	a	b	t	e	c	x

fast   jump   race

slow   smile   win

38

11 Read the text. Choose the correct words and write them next to 1—5.

> smiles   asks   am   are   says

"Haha, you can walk!"

says Hare, and ¹ __smiles__ .

"Yes. I ² _____ a tortoise," says

Tortoise. "I can walk."

"Then we can't have a race,"

³ _____ Hare.

"Why not?" ⁴ _____ Tortoise.

"You ⁵ _____ too slow," says Hare.

12 Ask and answer the questions with a friend. 💬

"Me, too slow? Then let's have a race," says Tortoise.

"OK! Let's run from here to the beach," says Hare.

"Great," says Tortoise.

1 *Who wants a race?*

Tortoise wants a race.

2 Who does he want a race with?

He wants a race . . .

3 Where do they want to race to?

They want to race to . . .

13 Talk about the two pictures with a friend. How are they different? Use the words in the box. 💬

> grass   jump   eat   sleep
>
> sun   race   run   win

a

b

> In picture a, Hare is jumping. In picture b, Hare isn't jumping, he is sleeping.

14 **Read the questions.**
Write the answers.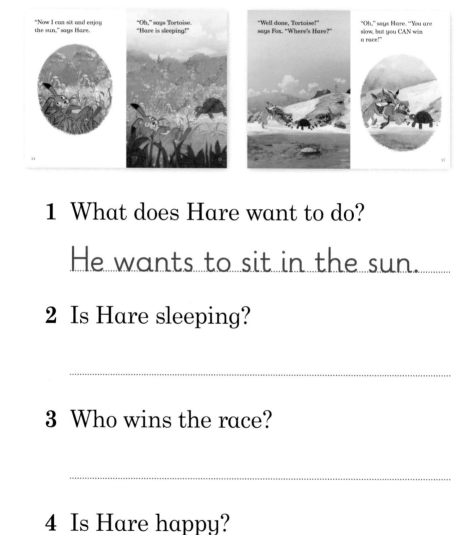

"Now I can sit and enjoy the sun," says Hare.

"Oh," says Tortoise. "Hare is sleeping!"

"Well done, Tortoise!" says Fox. "Where's Hare?"

"Oh," says Hare. "You are slow, but you CAN win a race!"

1 What does Hare want to do?

He wants to sit in the sun.

2 Is Hare sleeping?

....

3 Who wins the race?

....

4 Is Hare happy?

....

15 **Circle the correct pictures.**

1 He can jump and run fast.

 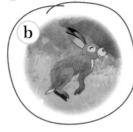 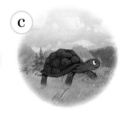

2 He is slow.

 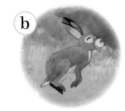 

3 Hare likes eating this.

4 Hare does not do this.

16 Put a ✓ by the things the animals do in the story. 📖

1   jump   ✓

2   eat grass   ☐

3   eat chocolate   ☐

4   play games   ☐

5   sit in the sun   ☐

6   sleep   ☐

7   smile   ☐

8   swim   ☐

9   race   ☐

10 run fast   ☐

11 walk   ☐

12 watch a race   ☐

13 watch TV   ☐

14 win a race   ☐

17 **Ask and answer the questions with a friend.**

1 Can you jump and run fast?

Yes, I can!

2 Who do you race with?

3 Where do you race?

4 Do you win?

18 **Order the story. Write 1—4.**

.... Tortoise wins the race.

.... Fox starts the race.

___1___ Hare jumps and runs.

.... Hare eats grass and sleeps.

19 **Look and read. Write the correct words in the boxes.** 📖 ✏️ ❓

eat grass   jump   go slow

sleep   walk   win the race

What Hare does	What Tortoise does
eat grass	

Ladybird 🐞 Readers

Visit **www.ladybirdeducation.co.uk**
for more FREE Ladybird Readers resources

✓ Digital edition
  of every title*

✓ Audio tracks (US/UK)

✓ Answer keys

✓ Lesson plans

✓ Role-plays

✓ Classroom
  display material

✓ Flashcards

✓ User guides

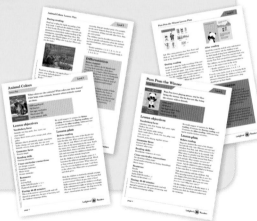

Register and sign up to the newsletter to receive your
FREE classroom resource pack!

*Ladybird Readers series only. Not applicable to *Peppa Pig* books.
Digital versions of Ladybird Readers books available once book has been purchased.